Santa's Secret

Adapted by James Ponti

Based on characters created by
Leo Benvenuti & Steve Rudnick

Based on the screenplay written by
Ed Decter & John J. Strauss

Produced by Brian Reilly, Bobby Newmyer,
Jeffrey Silver

Directed by Michael Lembeck

DISNEY
PRESS

New York

Printed in the United States of America

First Edition

1 3 5 7 9 10 8 6 4 2

Library of Congress Catalog Card Number: 2006925324

ISBN 1-4231-0507-9

Scott Calvin had an unusual job. He was Santa Claus. He lived at the North Pole with his wife, Carol. They were about to have a baby.

Carol needed help getting ready
for the baby. But Scott was too
busy. He was getting ready for
Christmas. Then, Carol had an
idea. Her parents could come to
the North Pole to help!

Curtis, one of the North Pole's top elves, was worried. Carol's parents did not know that Scott was Santa. They thought he ran a toy factory in Canada. Curtis thought that if they came to the North Pole, they might discover the S.O.S.—Secret of Santa.

But there was no choice. Curtis gave everyone the news. "Elves of the North Pole," he announced, "grab your hammers! The in-laws are coming!" They were going to keep Santa's secret safe.

The elves started making the
North Pole look like a town in
Canada to fool Carol's parents.
They even covered the tips of
their pointy ears so they wouldn't
look like elves.

Meanwhile, Scott took his sleigh to Minnesota, where Carol's parents lived. He brought along one of his magical friends—the Sandman. The Sandman could instantly put anyone to sleep.

When Scott and the Sandman arrived in Minnesota, Carol's father, Bud, was working in the garage. Bud was angry because his daughter never visited. He thought it was Scott's fault.

The Sandman asked Carol's
mom, Sylvia, why they had no
Christmas decorations. "We're not
big Christmas people," she
explained. The Sandman looked at
Scott. This was *not* going well.

Bud and Sylvia complained non-stop about *everything*. It was too much for the Sandman. It made him tired. Using his magic, he put them to sleep. Then he took a nap himself.

Luckily, the Sandman's magic
dust was very strong. Bud and
Sylvia slept through the *entire*
sleigh ride to the North Pole.

Scott landed in the main town.
"Welcome to Canada!" the elves
said when Bud and Sylvia finally
woke up.

Bud and Sylvia were confused. They didn't remember getting on an airplane. Scott explained that they had slept through the flight. Luckily, they believed him. So far, the plan was working. They did not know he was Santa!

Then Carol appeared. Bud was happy to see his daughter. He gave her a great big hug. So did Sylvia.

Scott and Carol showed Carol's parents around. The town looked Canadian. But Bud couldn't help noticing something unusual.
He looked closely at the elves.
"These people are short!" he said.

Scott got nervous. Bud could not
find out that the "Canadians"
were elves. So, Scott told Bud a
tiny little lie. He said Canadians
were just shorter than most
people.

Sylvia noticed something, too: Christmas was a *big* deal in Canada. Bud and Sylvia were noticing *too* much.

Curtis interrupted the tour.
He told Scott that there was a
problem. Scott was needed in the
factory.

Bud overheard Curtis and wanted
to see Scott's factory. This was
bad. If Bud saw the factory, he
might figure out Scott's secret.

They arrived at the factory. It was
a mess! There were all sorts of
problems. Scott was upset. Nothing
was going as planned.

It got worse. Bud saw the room where Carol was going to deliver her baby. It was too small! It was not good enough for his daughter *or* grandchild.

Bud took over the construction project. He told the worker elves what to do. He told them how to build a delivery room that was the *right* size.

Scott was angry. Bud was always picking on him! Scott was so upset, he didn't even help decorate the Christmas tree.

Finally, it was time for Christmas dinner. It was *supposed* to be nice. Scott stood up to give a toast, but he was interrupted.

Curtis called with more problems that *Santa* needed to solve. So *Scott* made everyone wait while he talked on the phone. It was hard pretending to be a normal guy. He had a holiday to run!

Bud did not like Scott being on the phone during dinner. He told Scott that he was too busy with work. Then he said something even worse. Bud said Scott was not being a good husband.

That was it! Scott had had enough. He threw up his hands, knocking over the Christmas tree.

Scott knew he had to stop fighting. He apologized to Bud. And Bud apologized, too. Then Scott said he had something special to show Bud and Sylvia.

Scott led Bud and Sylvia back
into the toy factory. But it looked
different. It was working! And
the elves were no longer covering
their ears! "We're not in Canada
anymore," Bud said to Sylvia.

Then Scott put on the big, red suit. It was time Bud and Sylvia knew the truth. They could not believe their eyes! Scott smiled. "You'll get used to it," he said.

The Secret of Santa was out—at least to Carol's parents. And the truth worked. Scott started to get along with Carol's parents. And when Carol had the baby, she named him Buddy. Buddy Claus. After her father.